THISTLE'S
MAGICALWHISTLE

——— THIS BOOK BELONGS TO ———

_____

DEEP IN THE HEART
    OF THE HICKORY FOREST
LIVED THISTLE THE ELF,
    AND HER BEST FRIEND HORACE.

NOW HORACE AND THISTLE
WERE TWO PEAS IN A POD,
BUT THE OTHERS THOUGHT
THAT THISTLE WAS ODD.

SEE, HORACE WAS BIG AND STRONG
AND FIT AS A FIDDLE,
WHILE THISTLE WAS SMALL
AND SCRAWNY AND LITTLE.

SHE HAD LONG CURLY HAIR
AND BIG BAGGY CLOTHES.
A CAP ON HER HEAD.
ROUND GLASSES ON HER NOSE.
THISTLE LIVED IN A LITTLE BROWN HOUSE IN
THE THICK OF THE WOOD.
SHE DIDN'T HAVE MANY FRIENDS
AND WAS MISUNDERSTOOD.

SEE THISTLE WAS DIFFERENT,
THE OTHERS WOULD SAY,
AND THEY WENT OFF TOGETHER
AND DIDN'T ASK HER TO PLAY.

THEY PLAYED IN THE WOOD
AND NEVER ASKED THISTLE.
THEY PRACTICED THEIR DANCE
AND PRACTICED THEIR WHISTLE.

THIS MADE THISTLE SAD.
    IT MADE THISTLE BLUE.   SO SHE MADE UP GAMES
MOST OF THE TIME SHE   IMAGINED IN HER HEAD.
    HAD NOTHING TO DO.   AND SOMETIMES JUST STARED
                                 AT THE CEILING
                         WHILE LYING IN BED.

BUT THAT BEAVER HORACE
    WAS THE BEST KIND OF FRIEND.
ON WEEKENDS TOGETHER
    THEY'D PLAY AND PRETEND:
CLIMBING TALL MOUNTAINS
    AND SAILING THE SEAS,
RIDING ON UNICORNS
    AND TAMING WILD BEES.
BUT THEN MONDAY WOULD COME
    AND IT WAS TIME FOR SCHOOL
AND THISTLE WOULD WORRY
    ABOUT THE THINGS SHE COULDN'T DO.

ON SCHOOL DAYS THEY PRACTICED
    THEIR WHISTLING EACH DAY,
AS EACH ONE PREPARED
    FOR THEIR ROLE IN THE CLASS PLAY.
WELL, EACH ONE BUT THISTLE,
    BECAUSE YOU SEE,
THISTLE NEEDED HELP.
    SHE LEARNED DIFFERENTLY.

NOW THISTLE WAS SMART,
   SMART AS CAN BE,
BUT SCHOOLWORK WAS HARD.
   IT DIDN'T COME NATURALLY.
NUMBERS WERE TWISTED.
   LETTERS BLURRED OUT.
SHE FELT OVERWHELMED
   AND WANTED TO SHOUT!
WRITING WASN'T EASY.
   NEITHER WAS MATH.
AND WHISTLING, FORGET IT!
   SHE'D RATHER PASS.

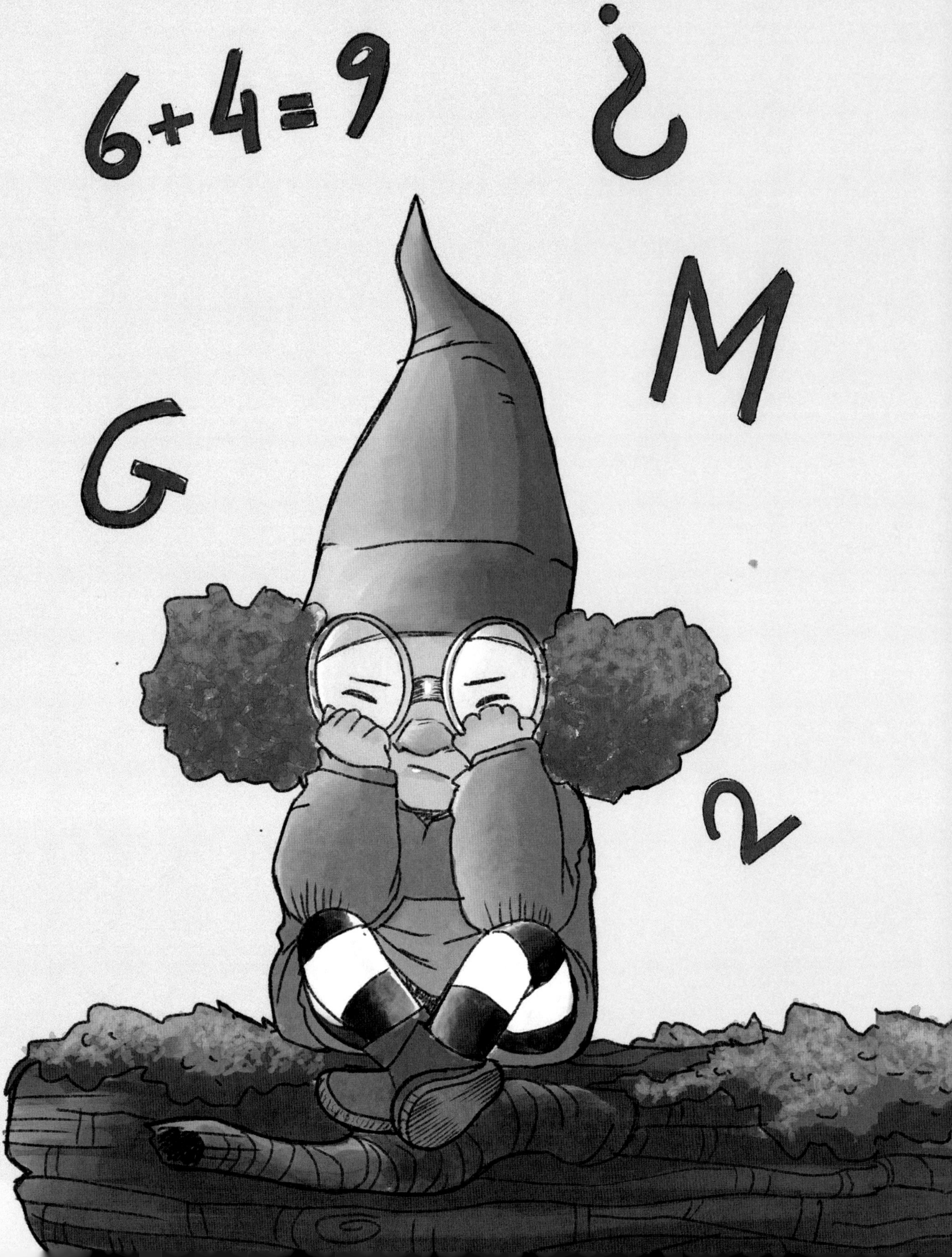
6+4=9
¿
M
G
2

"YOU CAN'T EVEN WHISTLE!"
    THE OTHERS WOULD TEASE.
"YOU CAN'T BE IN OUR PLAY."
    "GO HOME, THISTLE. LEAVE."
"THEY'RE RIGHT ABOUT ME. I CAN'T EVEN WHISTLE!
    I'LL NEVER BE GOOD,"
THOUGHT THE DISCOURAGED THISTLE.

BUT HORACE KNEW THISTLE
WAS CARING AND SMART.
HE KNEW THISTLE COULD DO IT.
SHE HAD LOTS OF HEART.
"C'MON THISTLE.
BELIEVE IN YOURSELF.
I KNOW YOU CAN WHISTLE
AND I'M HERE TO HELP."

"JUST PUCKER YOUR LIPS
    AND HOLD DOWN YOUR TONGUE.
THEN TAKE A DEEP BREATH
    AND EMPTY YOUR LUNGS."
THISTLE DID EXACTLY
    AS HORACE HAD SAID,
BUT NOTHING HAPPENED,
    JUST AS SHE DREAD.
"I CAN'T EVEN DO IT.
    I'VE HAD IT! I'VE TRIED!"
SHE SAT DOWN ON A STUMP
    AND STARTED TO CRY.

HORACE AND THISTLE WORKED HARD
EVERY DAY.
HORACE NEVER LOST PATIENCE
AND SHOWED THISTLE THE WAY.

LITTLE BY LITTLE AND BIT BY BIT,
        HORACE HELPED THISTLE
TO PUCKER HER LIPS,
        AND HOLD DOWN HER TONGUE,
AND BLOW A BIG BLOW,
        AND BEFORE THISTLE KNEW IT,
WHAT DO YOU KNOW!

A BEAUTIFUL SOUND. A MAGICAL THING!
THISTLE WAS WHISTLING! THISTLE COULD SING!
HER EYES THEY LIT UP
AND HER CONFIDENCE GREW,
AS SHE WHISTLED ALOUD A BEAUTIFUL TUNE.

THE NEXT DAY INTO CLASS
    WALKED A CONFIDENT THISTLE.
SHE KNEW SHE COULD DO IT.
    SHE KNEW HOW TO WHISTLE.
BUT THE OTHER KIDS GROANED,
    "JUST GO ON HOME."
"GET OUT OF HERE, THISTLE."
    "LEAVE US ALONE."
SHE TURNED TOWARD THE DOOR
    TO HEAD BACK TO THE FOREST.
BUT THEN CAME A TAP ON THE SHOULDER
    FROM HER BEST BUDDY, HORACE.

"DON'T LISTEN TO THEM.
    YOU KNOW HOW TO WHISTLE.
JUST LIKE WE PRACTICED.
    NOW SHOW THEM, THISTLE."
THISTLE PICKED UP HER CHIN,
    WIPED THE TEAR FROM HER EYE.
SHE PUFFED UP HER CHEST,
    AND HELD HER HEAD HIGH.

SHE FIRST PUCKERED HER LIPS,
   THEN SHE HELD DOWN HER TONGUE,
THEN BLEW A BIG BLOW
   AND OUT CAME A WHISTLE, WHAT DO YOU KNOW!
IT WAS A BEAUTIFUL SOUND.
   IT WAS A MAGICAL THING!

THISTLE WAS WHISTLING!
THISTLE COULD SING!
HER EYES LIT UP,
AND HER CONFIDENCE GREW,
AS SHE WHISTLED ALOUD
A BEAUTIFUL TUNE.

About the Author:

Jeff Michaelson is the Author of Thistle's Magical Whistle.
This is Jeff's first children's book, inspired by his daughter,
Lindsey, a self-proclaimed "quirky kid' who's struggled
with social anxiety and learning challenges most of her life.
Jeff's hope is that this book helps parents and children
understand what it's like to feel different and how friendship
and just a little bit of patience can make a huge
difference in someone's life.

Learn more and access resources check out
www.thistletheelf.com

Thistle's Magical Whistle
Copyrights 2020 © Jeff Michaelson

ISBN 978-0-578-72999-2

Story by Jeff Michaelson
Illustrations by Francesca Da Sacco
Graphic Design by Gabriel B. Pagani

Font Type: Bear Hugs by Ratticassin

Made in the USA
Coppell, TX
09 October 2020